Original Korean text by Cecil Kim
Illustrations by Chiara Dattola
Original Korean edition © Yeowon Media Co. Ltd.

This English edition published by big & SMALL in 2015
by arrangement with Yeowon Media Co. Ltd.
English text edited by Joy Cowley
English edition © big & SMALL 2015

Distributed in the United States and Canada by
Lerner Publishing Group, Inc.
241 First Avenue North
Minneapolis, MN 55401 U.S.A.
www.lernerbooks.com

ISBN: 978-1-925186-40-6

Printed in the United States of America

1 – CG – 5/31/15

One Little Bean

Written by Cecil Kim Illustrated by Chiara Dattola
Edited by Joy Cowley

One little bean
fell on the ground.
Ping!

6

"I'm scared!"
cried the little bean.

8

10

The good earth said,
"Don't be scared, little bean.
I will cover you with my blanket."

11

The cloud said, "It's okay.
I will look after you
with cool, soft rain."

The bugs in the earth said,
"Don't worry, little bean.
We will be your friends."

Pop! Out of the little bean,
came a green shoot.
It grew up through the earth.

"What will happen to me?"
cried the little bean.

The sun smiled and said,
"Don't worry, little bean.
I will shine my light on you!"

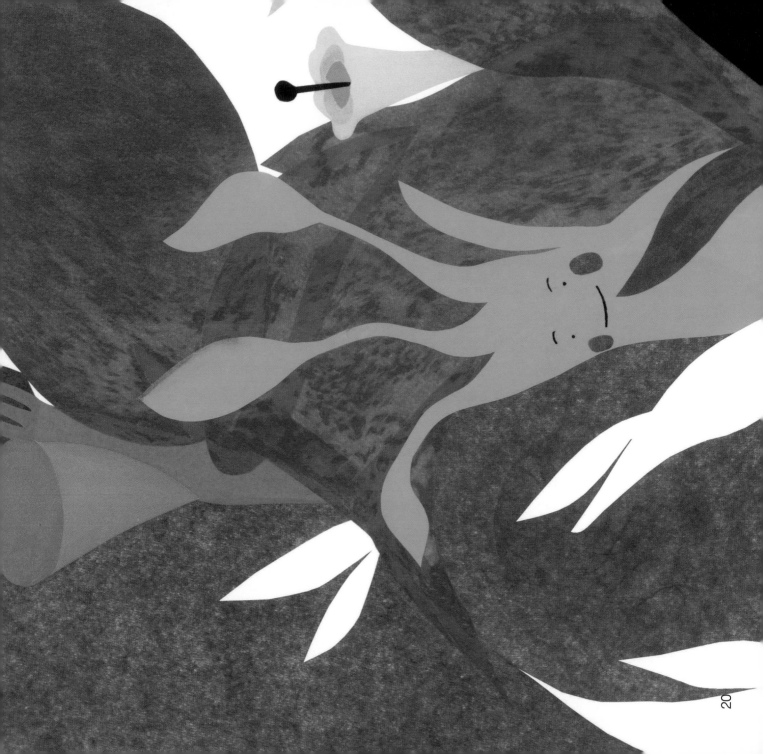

The wind whispered,
"I will blow my gentle breath
on your green leaves."

"Hello, little bean!"
said the bee and the butterfly.
"We will sing and dance for you."

The little bean
grew long pods.

The child said, "Look!
The bean pods are opening!"

Ping! Ping! Ping!

More little beans!